Show Some Respect

by Anastasia Suen
illustrated by Jeff Ebbeler

Content Consultant:
Vicki F. Panaccione, Ph.D.
Licensed Child Psychologist
Founder, Better Parenting Institute

visit us at
www.abdopublishing.com

Published by Red Wagon, a division of the ABDO Publishing Group, 8000 West 78th Street, Edina, Minnesota, 55439.

Printed in the United States.

Text by Anastasia Suen
Illustrations by Jeff Ebbeler
Edited by Patricia Stockland
Interior layout and design by Becky Daum
Cover design by Becky Daum

Library of Congress Cataloging-in-Publication Data

Suen, Anastasia.
Show some respect / Anastasia Suen ; illustrated by Jeffery Ebbeler.
p. cm. -- (Main Street school)
Summary: Isaiah explains to Jack why cleaning up after himself shows respect for himself and the janitor.
ISBN-13: 978-1-60270-033-8
[1. Respect--Fiction. 2. Schools--Fiction.] I. Ebbeler, Jeffrey, ill. II. Title.
PZ7.S94343Sh 2007

[E]--dc22

2007004719

"That was a great assembly," said Miss K when they came back to class. "Now it's time to go home. Let's pick up the trash around our desks."

"Why do we have to do that?" asked Jack. "That's the janitor's job."

"You say that every day," said Isaiah. He reached under his desk. "Only three scraps here."

"Well, it is his job," said Jack.

"But you're the one who dropped the trash," said Isaiah.

"So what?" asked Jack. "It's not my job to clean it up."

"Why not?" asked Isaiah.

"We're done!" said the kids in row three.
They all raised their hands.

Miss K walked down their row.

"Very clean," said Miss K. "Put up your chairs and line up."

The kids in row three put their chairs on top of their desks.

"That's another thing," said Jack. "Why do we have to put up the chairs?"

"We always put up the chairs," said Isaiah. "Hey, you missed one." He pointed at a scrap of paper under Jack's desk.

"Not another one," said Jack. He bent over and picked the paper up.

"We're done!" said the kids in
row two. They all raised
their hands.

Miss K walked down their row.

"Looks good," said Miss K.
"Put up your chairs and line up."

"We're never going to get out
of here," said Jack.

"Not if you don't hurry up,"
said Isaiah. "Everyone else
is done."

“I’m done,” said Jack.

Miss K walked down their row.
“Not quite,” she said. “There’s
paper falling out of your desk.”

“Oh,” said Jack.
He pushed in the paper.

“Now you’re ready,” said Miss K.
“Put up your chairs and line up.”

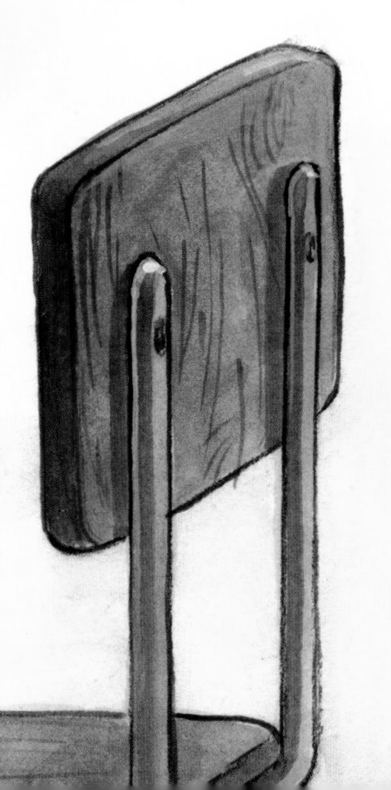

Jack stood up and put the chair on his desk.

"I still don't know why we have to do all
this work."

"It's our classroom," said Isaiah.

"I don't have to clean at home," said Jack.
"Why should I do it here?"

"You don't clean your room?" asked Isaiah. He picked up his backpack.

"No way," said Jack.

"Does it look like your desk?" asked Isaiah.

"Uh," said Jack. He thought about the papers in his desk and his messy room at home. "Well..."

"I thought so," said Isaiah.

Jack put on his backpack.
"There's nothing wrong with my desk."

"You can't find anything in there," said Isaiah.

"Yes, I can," said Jack.

"Then why did you borrow a pencil *and* a pen from me today?" asked Isaiah.

"Well...," said Jack.

The bell rang.

"Come on," said Isaiah. "Now we can go play basketball."

Jack and Isaiah walked to the gym.

"Hi, Coach," said Isaiah.

"Hi, Coach," said Jack.

"Hi, boys," said Coach. He put a mark by their names on his clipboard.

Soon all of the kids for After School Sports were there.

"Now we can play," said Jack. "It's about time!"

Whirrrr...

"What's that sound?" asked Jack. He turned around.

It was the janitor with the sweeper machine. He was cleaning the floor.

Coach looked up and waved. The janitor waved back.

"It looks like Mr. Hank is going to be in the gym for a while," said Coach.

"Let's go outside," said Coach.

"Not now!" said Jack.

"I thought you liked to go
outside," said Isaiah.

"But I wanted to play basketball,"
said Jack.

"Let's go, boys," said Coach.
He opened the door.

"That janitor is nothing but
trouble," said Jack.

"What?" asked Isaiah.

"Why can't he clean the right things?" asked Jack.

"What does *that* mean?" asked Isaiah as they walked out the door.

"It means he should clean our classroom," said Jack, "and let us play ball."

"Did you forget about the assembly we had this afternoon?" asked Isaiah.

"What does that have to do with it?" asked Jack.

"They didn't make anyone clean before they left," said Isaiah. "We can't play basketball with all of that trash on the floor."

"Oh," said Jack.

"Quit being so mean, and show some respect," said Isaiah. "He's making the gym clean for us."

"Okay," said Jack. "I get it. But that still doesn't mean I like to clean."

Isaiah laughed. "I already knew that!"

What Do You Think?

1. Why does Miss K make the class clean before they go home?

2. How does Jack feel about cleaning up after himself?

3. How do you think Isaiah feels about Jack's comments?

4. How could Jack show more respect to the janitor?

Words to Know

fair—reasonable and just.
polite—having good manners, being well behaved and courteous to others.
positive—helpful or constructive; having a good attitude.
reliable—trustworthy or dependable; people can count on you.
respect—a feeling of admiration or consideration for someone that makes you take the person seriously.

Miss K's Classroom Rules

1. Be polite.
2. Be fair.
3. Be reliable.
4. Be positive.

Web Sites

To learn more about respect, visit ABDO Publishing Company on the World Wide Web at **www.abdopublishing.com**. Web sites about respect are featured on our Book Links page. These links are routinely monitored and updated to provide the most current information available.